Smithsonian Prehistoric Zone

Apatosaurus

by Gerry Bailey
Illustrated by Trevor Reaveley

Crabtree Publishing Company

www.crabtreebooks.com

Crabtree Publishing Company

www.crabtreebooks.com

Author
Gerry Bailey

Illustrator
Trevor Reaveley

Editorial coordinator
Kathy Middleton

Editor
Lynn Peppas

Proofreaders
Crystal Sikkens
Kathy Middleton

Prepress technician
Samara Parent

Print and production coordinator
Katherine Berti

Library of Congress Cataloging-in-Publication Data

Bailey, Gerry.
Apatosaurus / by Gerry Bailey ; illustrated by Trevor Reaveley.
    p. cm. -- (Smithsonian prehistoric zone)
Includes index.
ISBN 978-0-7787-1811-6 (pbk. : alk. paper) -- ISBN 978-0-7787-1798-0 (reinforced library binding : alk. paper) -- ISBN 978-1-4271-9702-3 (electronic (pdf))
1. Apatosaurus--Juvenile literature. I. Reaveley, Trevor, ill. II. Title.

QE862.S3B35 2011
567.913'8--dc22

2010044025

Library and Archives Canada Cataloguing in Publication

Bailey, Gerry
    Apatosaurus / by Gerry Bailey ; illustrated by
Trevor Reavely.

(Smithsonian prehistoric zone)
Includes index.
At head of title: Smithsonian Institution.
Issued also in electronic format.
ISBN 978-0-7787-1798-0 (bound).-- ISBN 978-0-7787-1811-6 (pbk.)

1. Apatosaurus--Juvenile literature. I. Reaveley, Trevor
II. Smithsonian Institution III. Title. IV. Series: Bailey,
Gerry. Smithsonian prehistoric zone.

QE862.S3B33 2011   j567.913'8   C2010-906882-3

Crabtree Publishing Company

www.crabtreebooks.com   1-800-387-7650
Copyright © **2011 CRABTREE PUBLISHING COMPANY**.
All rights reserved. No part of this publication may be reproduced, stored in a retrieval system or be transmitted in any form or by any means, electronic, mechanical, photocopying, recording, or otherwise, without the prior written permission of Crabtree Publishing Company. In Canada: we acknowledge the financial support of the Government of Canada through the Canada Book Fund for our publishing activities.

Published in the United States
Crabtree Publishing
PMB 59051
350 Fifth Avenue, 59th Floor
New York, New York 10118

Published in Canada
Crabtree Publishing
616 Welland Ave.
St. Catharines, Ontario
L2M 5V6

Printed in China/012011/GW20101014

Dinosaurs

Living things had been around for billions of years before dinosaurs came along. Animal life on Earth started with single-cell **organisms** that lived in the seas. About 380 million years ago, some animals came out of the sea and onto the land. These were the ancestors that would become the mighty dinosaurs.

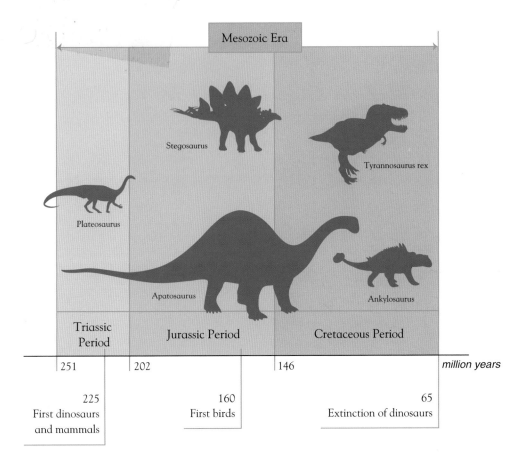

The dinosaur era is called the Mesozoic era. It is divided into three parts called the Triassic, Jurassic, and Cretaceous periods. During the Jurassic period the climate was warm and plenty of rain fell. Plant-eating dinosaurs, such as *Apatosaurus* and *Brachiosaurus*, fed on ferns, horsetails, cycad leaves, and cones from pine trees. Meat-eaters, such as *Allosaurus* and *Ceratosaurus*, fed on the plant-eaters and each other.

Apatosaurus walked carefully toward the stream. She was a long-necked dinosaur who lived hundreds of millions of years ago. Her feet began to sink into the marshy soil as she approached the stream. The soft ground could not support her great weight. If she was not careful, she would sink into the mud and become stuck.

Apatosaurus was a plant-eater.
The delicious plants she liked
to eat grew by the stream.

There were ferns and horsetails
close to the ground. There were
fern-like cycads too.

Apatosaurus felt more tired than usual. It was not just the heat. She was used to that as it was always warm and humid. Her tiredness was due to something quite different. She was full of eggs and would soon be **shedding** them.

Across the stream she could see a small herd
of giant, slow-moving plant-eaters called
Brachiosaurus. There was an Allosaurus too.
It was a dangerous **predator**. There was only
one Allosaurus, however. One could not harm
a large herd. The Allosaurus would
be a greater danger if there had
only been one Brachiosaurus.
Apatosaurus knew it was
time to move away.

She backed away from the stream and headed
slowly for the forest nearby. Her meal was
finished for now. She did not like the look of
the Allosaurus. She had sensed it was hungry.

She felt safer at the edge of the forest, especially in her condition. Apatosaurus stretched her long neck into the trees and nibbled on some leafy cycads.

Apatosaurus had to eat a great deal of plant food to get enough energy to satisfy her large body. Now she gave her full attention to the meal. The sound of insects buzzing around her

and the tearing sound made as she pulled at the
leaves were the only noises she could hear. She
was not aware of another more threatening sound.
Apatosaurus did not know she was being watched.

As Apatosaurus fed, a pack of **carnivorous** Ceratosaurus had sneaked up behind her. They were spreading out to surround her. These small predator dinosaurs were hungry. Could they take on Apatosaurus?

Suddenly she realized it was too quiet.
Apatosaurus pulled her head from the forest
and turned around. The Ceratosaurus stared
at her hungrily. Their curved teeth glinted.

The band of Ceratosaurus watched their **prey**. They could see that she was walking more slowly than usual. She was heavy with eggs. This made her easy prey because she was not with the rest of her herd.

The horn-snouted Ceratosaurus worked as
a team. Usually they would not attack such
a big dinosaur. They sensed she was in a
weak state. They might have a chance.

The Ceratosaurus attacked as if their leader had given them a silent order. Apatosaurus knew how to defend herself. She lashed her tail at the attacking predators. She hit one and knocked it over. Her tail flew back and forth like a huge whip. The Ceratosaurus tumbled over, yelping in pain.

It was no use. Apatosaurus might be on her own, but her flailing tail was too powerful a weapon for them to handle. The Ceratosaurus backed off and soon ran away. They would need to search for easier prey. Apatosaurus bent her great neck and looked at her body. She had received a few scratches, but they would heal. She shuffled away from the scene of the attack, stopping to rest as often as she could.

At last Apatosaurus found what she was looking for.
Her tiredness and slowness had been for a reason.
Inside her body she was carrying precious eggs. She had
built a nest the previous day and now she stood over it.

Slowly and gently, she lowered her legs
and tail over the nest. A huge egg fell
into it. She continued to lay her eggs
until there were 12 in the nest.

The nest Apatosaurus built for her eggs was
a dug-out hole in the soil. She filled it with
plants that would **rot** over time. These
would give off heat like a **compost** heap.

She would stay and protect her babies for a few weeks after they hatched. Then she would move off again. Their **instinct** would help them **survive** on their own.

All about Apatosaurus

(a-PAT-oh-SAW-russ)

The *Apatosaurus* lived around 150 million years ago during the **Jurassic** period. *Apatosaurus* used to be called *Brontosaurus*, or "thunder lizard." It was one of the largest land animals ever to have lived. It was about 70 feet (21 meters) long. It weighed 33 tons (30 metric tons), and was as tall as a three-storey building.

The most amazing features of the *Apatosaurus* were its neck and tail. Its neck was 20 feet (6 meters) long and its tail was 30 feet (9 meters) long. Its long neck allowed it to reach high up into the trees of the forest for leaves. Its tail was made up of 82 connected **vertebrae** and could be used as a fearsome whipping weapon. It had a pair of bony plates on the underside of its tail that protected the soft part from wear when the tail was dragged along the ground.

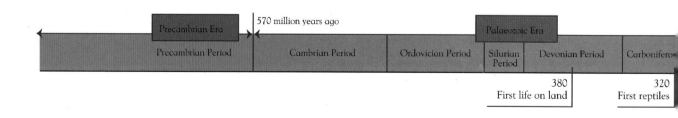

570 million years ago

Precambrian Era			Palaeozoic Era		
Precambrian Period	Cambrian Period	Ordovician Period	Silurian Period	Devonian Period	Carbonifero...

380
First life on land

320
First reptiles

Even though *Apatosaurus* was huge it had a very small head. Inside was a small brain about the size of a large apple. It had long, thin, peg-like teeth that were not very strong. New teeth would grow to replace the old ones when they were worn out. *Apatosaurus* probably used its teeth to rake leaves from branches.

Apatosaurus had short, stout legs underneath its body. Five toes grew on each foot. There was a claw on the big toe of each front foot that it could have used as a weapon. There were three claws on each back foot. It could rear up on its hind legs to fight off predators.

Apatosaurus lived a long life for a dinosaur. Some may have lived as long as 50 years.

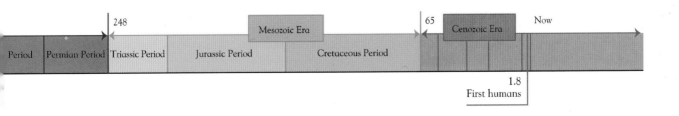

| Period | Permian Period | Triassic Period | Jurassic Period | Cretaceous Period | | Cenozoic Era | Now |

248

Mesozoic Era

65

1.8
First humans

Dinosaur eggs

Dinosaurs, such as *Apatosaurus* and *Maiasaura*, did not give birth to live young as **mammals** do. Instead they laid eggs just like reptiles do today. They would make a nest by digging a hole in the ground. The eggs would be laid in the nest.

Some dinosaurs made nests in groups or colonies. They probably did this as protection against predators. The *Maiasaura* is a plant-eating dinosaur whose name means "good mother lizard." The group made their nests about 23 feet (7 meters) apart to prevent the eggs from being crushed by other adult *Maiasaura*. The nests were still close enough to protect them against egg-hunting dinosaurs.

Huge dinosaurs such as *Apatosaurus* were too big to sit on the eggs to keep them warm until they hatched. Instead they covered them with earth or sand. Other dinosaurs, such as *Orodromeus*, covered their eggs with a mixture of rotting vegetation and sand.

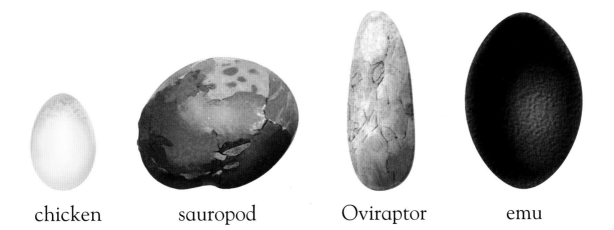

chicken   sauropod   Oviraptor   emu

Dinosaur eggs were small and fragile. The shell had to be thin enough to let oxygen through the **pores** to the baby inside, and also allow the baby to break out.

Some **hatchlings** could move as soon as they hatched. Others were too small and weak and had to stay in the nest and be looked after by adult dinosaurs.

Stones in her stomach

Apatosaurus shared a way of **digesting** food that is used by birds we see today. Birds have a muscular sack, called a gizzard, as part of their stomach. Inside the gizzard are small stones or grit that the bird has swallowed. The stones or grit help to crush the food they eat before it goes into the **intestines**.

Scientists have found similar small stones or pebbles among the bones of some plant-eating dinosaurs. They believe these stones were used the same way. Pebbles like this that help animals digest are called gastroliths. They become polished and smooth from grinding up food.

Dinosaurs that used gastroliths probably swallowed quite a lot of them. A *Barosaurus* was a 79-foot- (24-meter-) long planteating dinosaur. Its skeleton was found in North America with 64 polished stones between its ribs. When birds have worn out their stones they bring them up and swallow replacements. Plant-eating dinosaurs that used gastroliths probably did the same thing.

Glossary

carnivorous Feeding on other animals' flesh

compost A mixture of dead and decaying plant matter

digest To break down and change food so that it can be absorbed by the body

hatchling An animal that is born from an egg

instinct A natural feeling or ability that an animal is born with

intestine A long tube inside the body that helps digest food

mammal Warm-blooded animals that have a backbone

organisms Any living animal or plant

pore A very small hole that allows air or liquid to go through

predator An animal that hunts other animals

prey An animal that is hunted by another animal

rot To decompose or break down

shed To eject or give off from the body

survive To live

vertebrae The bones that make up the backbone of an animal

Index

Further Reading and Websites

Field Guide to Dinosaurs by Steve Brusatte. Book Sales, Inc. (2009)

Apatosaurus by Susan Heinrichs Gray and Robert Squier. Child's World (2009)

Websites:

www.smithsonianeducation.org

www.enchantedlearning.com/subjects/dinosaurs